One-Shoe's
Wishes

Illustrated by
Andrew McLean

HAPPY CAT BOOKS

Meet the mice who live in Squeak Street

Old Bun lives in Number One.
His piles of gold shine like the sun.

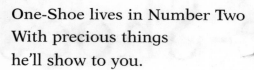

One-Shoe lives in Number Two
With precious things
he'll show to you.

Fee-Fee lives in Number Three
With her enormous family.

Pink-Paw lives in Number Four.
She paints until her paws are sore.

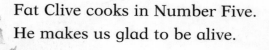

Fat Clive cooks in Number Five.
He makes us glad to be alive.

Quick-Sticks lives in Number Six.
Her band is called the Squeaky Chicks.

Kevin lives in Number Seven.
He thinks old cars
are simply heaven.

Tails the Great, in Number Eight,
Spooks us into an awful state.

Adeline, in Number Nine,
Builds boats — all to her own design.

And post-mouse Ben, in Number Ten,
Is resting his poor feet again.

Published by
Happy Cat Books
An imprint of Catnip Publishing Ltd
Islington Business Centre
3-5 Islington High Street
London N1 9LQ

First published in Australia 2006 by Working Title Press,
33 Balham Avenue, Kingswood, SA 5062

This edition first published 2007
1 3 5 7 9 10 8 6 4 2

A CIP catalogue record for this book is available
from the British Library

ISBN 978-1-905117-52-9

Printed in Poland

www.catnippublishing.co.uk

Contents

~

Chapter 1
~
One-Shoe

One-Shoe loved things that were old and strange. He loved finding them, then cleaning them up to sell in his little shop at Number Two Squeak Street.

One-Shoe loved his work so much that he found it hard to think about anything else.

He forgot to clean his house.
He forgot to brush his whiskers.
Sometimes he even forgot to eat.

He usually remembered to get dressed in the morning, but his house was so messy that often he only found one shoe to put on.

That was why he was called One-Shoe. His real name was Desmond, but he'd forgotten that long ago.

His shop was famous, and so
was he. Mice came from all over
Mouseville to buy things from
One-Shoe.

When they met him for the first time, they were surprised. They wondered how such a quiet, forgetful mouse had been able to find so many amazing treasures.

But his friends in Squeak Street knew only too well. They knew the other side of One-Shoe — One-Shoe the fearless treasure hunter.

Every now and then, One-Shoe
locked his shop and set off on a
treasure hunt.

His trips took him to strange,
wild places, far from home.

Many times he had risked his life battling steep cliffs, deep rivers and terrible monsters. He never gave up.

How else had he snatched the Crown of a Thousand Stars from the Snails of Doom?

Or saved the famous Silver Sword from the Deep Dark Pool?

One-Shoe loved his life. He didn't have a worry in the world.

Until, one day, he found the most amazing thing of all.

Chapter 2

~

The Bottle

One morning, One-Shoe arrived home after a long and dangerous trip. He was tired, but very happy. His sack was full of treasure.

Friends who saw him shouted and waved, but One-Shoe didn't stop to chat. He was longing to start work on the things he had found.

Safe in his work room at last, he opened his sack. The first thing he pulled out was a dirty sock with a large lump in the toe.

He stared at it, puzzled. Then he remembered. While hiding from a gang of rats, he'd found a funny little bottle. He'd put it in the sock to stop it getting broken.

He took the bottle out of the
sock, and looked at it.

It was thick with dust. It was
round at the bottom, and it had a
long, smooth neck with a glass
stopper at the top.

Carefully, One-Shoe began to wash it. As the dust floated away he saw that it was a great treasure indeed. It was blue as the sky. On the front was a picture of a rose.

One-Shoe lifted the bottle from the water and began to rub it dry.

Then something very strange happened. The stopper at the top of the bottle began to jiggle up and down — all by itself.

Amazed, One-Shoe tugged it gently. The stopper sprang out with a loud POP!

And from the neck of the bottle gushed a stream of bright pink smoke.

One-Shoe yelled, and jumped back. He tripped over his own feet and sat down hard on the floor.

The smoke swirled in a fat cloud over the top of the bottle. Then, suddenly, a rather plump mouse wearing baggy pale blue pants was sitting on the table.

"Greetings, Master!" said the plump mouse. "I am Edam, the genie of the bottle. What do you wish?"

One-Shoe's mouth fell open.

"Don't just sit there," snapped Edam. "Get on with it! I don't want to hang around this dump any longer than I have to. No offence."

Chapter 3

~

Edam

"I don't understand," One-Shoe gulped.

Edam yawned and brushed a speck of dust from his orange silk shoe.

"You set me free," he said. "So you have to make three wishes before I can leave. Wishes just for you, not for anyone else. Those are the rules. So — what do you want?"

Slowly One-Shoe got to his feet. "I — I don't know," he said.

Edam looked at him coldly. "What about a new house?" he said. "This place is a hole. No offence."

"I like my house!" exclaimed One-Shoe. "I don't want a new one."

Edam shrugged. "Gold, then," he said. "The Genie Handbook says that nine out of ten Masters wish for gold. Boring, but true."

"I don't want gold," cried One-Shoe. "I have plenty to live on. Extra cheese just takes up space."

Edam sighed and wiggled his ears. A large bowl of chocolate chip cookies appeared in his hand.

He crammed three cookies into his mouth and chewed gloomily.

"I always eat when I'm depressed," he mumbled. "Look, just make a wish, will you? There must be something you'd like."

"I'd like someone to do the washing-up," said One-Shoe. "I forgot to do it before I went away, and now it smells a bit."

Edam seemed to swell to twice his size. "The washing-up!" he yelled, spitting crumbs all over his baggy pants. "What do you think I am, a maid?"

He grabbed more cookies and stuffed them so far into his mouth that he nearly choked.

One-Shoe pounded him on the back.

"I've never been so insulted in my life," sniffed Edam. His eyes began to water.

"Don't cry!" begged One-Shoe, horrified. "Look, forget about the washing-up. I'll think of something else. My friends will help."

He hurried to the front door.

"Don't you tell them about me,"
Edam called after him. "That's
against the rules too."

"I won't give up," One-Shoe muttered to himself. "I'll think of three wishes, even if I have to talk to every mouse in Squeak Street to do it!"

He threw open the door and ran out into the street.

Chapter 4

~

Questions

Outside, he nearly crashed into Old Bun from Number One, who was slowly hobbling by.

"Old Bun!" gasped One-Shoe. "Can you tell me what you'd wish for, if the wish was just for yourself?"

"Why, bless my whiskers, I'd wish to be young again," said Old Bun.

One-Shoe remembered being young. His mother and father hadn't liked him finding strange old things and bringing them home.

"Why don't you find something useful, like cheese?" his father always grumbled.

"Why don't you tidy your room,
and find your other shoe?" his
mother always complained.

"No," One-Shoe said to himself.
"I don't want to be young again."

Fee-Fee, the busy mother from Number Three, said that she'd wish for a holiday. But One-Shoe loved his work. He didn't want a holiday.

Pink-Paw, the happy artist from Number Four, said she'd like to travel to faraway places. But One-Shoe didn't need to wish for that. He went to faraway places all the time.

Clive, the cook from Number Five, said he'd wish to be thinner, and still eat lots of cake. But One-Shoe didn't need to be thinner. His walking trips kept him slim.

Quick-Sticks, the drummer from Number Six, said that she'd like her band to be famous. But One-Shoe was famous already — as famous as he wanted to be, anyway.

Kevin from Number Seven said that he'd wish for a pale blue Thunderbird. "It's a special kind of old car," he explained. "The best!"

But One-Shoe didn't need a car.
There were no roads in the wild
places he visited.

He tried to creep past the door of Number Eight Squeak Street, but it flew open as he passed.

There stood Tails the Great, the spooky magic mouse, holding a spoon that dripped with green slime.

One-Shoe backed away. "Um...
can you tell me what you'd wish
for, if the wish was just for
yourself?" he mumbled.

Tails the Great's eyes glittered.
"I'd wish to rule the world!" he
said.

One-Shoe moved quickly on. He didn't want to rule the world. If he did that, he'd have no time to do anything else!

Adeline, the boat maker from Number Nine, was visiting Ben the post-mouse, who lived in the last house of all. Ben was soaking his sore feet in a bowl of water.

Adeline said she'd wish for an extra pair of hands, to help her make her boats more quickly. Ben said he'd like new feet — feet without blisters.

But One-Shoe didn't want an extra pair of hands, or new feet. The ones he had worked perfectly well.

So he walked on home. He'd asked everyone, and he still didn't have a wish. Not one.

Chapter 5
~
Three Wishes

When One-Shoe got home, Edam
was still sitting on the work room
table. The cookie bowl was empty.

"Well? Have you got a wish
yet?" Edam snapped.

"No, I haven't," sighed One-
Shoe. "There's nothing I want."

Edam groaned and wiggled his ears. Jam tarts appeared in the bowl. He gobbled two miserably.

"Just my luck to get a stupid Master who's happy the way he is!" he said.

And suddenly One-Shoe had a wonderful idea.

"You're right!" he yelled. "I'm happy the way I am. So, are you ready? Three wishes coming up!"

Edam stared, his cheeks bulging.

"I wish to live where I live now, for as long as I want to," said One-Shoe. "And I wish to do the work I do now, for as long as I want to. And I wish to have the friends I have now, for as long as they want to stay."

Edam looked disgusted. "Those
aren't proper wishes!" he said.

"Yes they are!" said One-Shoe.
"They're what I want most in the
world. Who's the Master around
here, anyway?"

Edam shrugged and wiggled his ears three times. "Done!" he said sulkily. "Now you can live in this boring hole, and spend your time hunting old rubbish, for as long as you like."

"Good!" said One-Shoe. "Thank you and goodbye."

"What the other genies will say about this I do not know," muttered Edam. "Oh, the shame of it!"

He crammed the rest of the jam tarts into his mouth. Then he disappeared in a puff of pink smoke.

One-Shoe breathed a sigh of relief. He put the stopper back in the little blue bottle. He took the bottle into the shop and placed it in the window, where it shone like a small blue star.

"Excellent!" said One-Shoe, and he hurried back to work.

On the way, he forgot to watch where he was going. He tripped over some mess, and stubbed his bare toe.

At that moment, three new wishes came into One-Shoe's mind. A better memory. A tidy house. And a new shoe.

"Oh, why didn't I think of those before?" he groaned.

Then he remembered what he had wished for, and he smiled.

He was very happy with things just the way they were.